IN THE ORCHARD

&

THREE PICTURES

&

EVENING OVER SUSSEX:
REFLECTIONS IN A MOTOR CAR

IN THE SAME SERIES

How Should One Read a Book?
Kew Gardens
On Being Ill

IN THE GOLD-FOILED
VIRGINIA WOOLF COLLECTION

A Room of One's Own
Mrs Dalloway
To the Lighthouse

In the Orchard

VIRGINIA WOOLF

RENARD PRESS

RENARD PRESS LTD

124 City Road
London EC1V 2NX
United Kingdom
info@renardpress.com
020 8050 2928

www.renardpress.com

'In the Orchard' first published in 1923; 'Three Pictures' and 'Evening Over Sussex: Reflections in a Motor Car' first published in 1942.
This edition first published by Renard Press Ltd in 2024

Edited text, Notes and Selection © Renard Press Ltd, 2024

Cover design by Will Dady
Extra Material edited by Tom Conaghan

Printed on FSC-accredited papers in the UK by 4edge Limited

ISBN: 978-1-80447-095-4

9 8 7 6 5 4 3 2 1

CLIMATE POSITIVE Renard Press is proud to be a climate positive publisher, removing more carbon from the air than we emit and planting a small forest. For more information see renardpress.com/eco.

All rights reserved. This publication may not be reproduced, stored in a retrieval system or transmitted, in any form or by any means – electronic, mechanical, photocopying, recording or otherwise – without the prior permission of the publisher.

CONTENTS

In the Orchard   3

Three Pictures   17

Evening Over Sussex   27

Notes   35

A Biographical Note on
Virginia Woolf   37

IN THE ORCHARD

MIRANDA SLEPT in the orchard, lying in a long chair beneath the apple tree. Her book had fallen into the grass, and her finger still seemed to point at the sentence '*Ce pays est vraiment un des coins du monde oui le rire des filles eclate le mieux…*'* as if she had fallen asleep just there. The opals on her finger flushed green, flushed rosy and again flushed orange as the sun, oozing through the apple trees, filled them. Then, when the breeze blew, her purple dress rippled like a flower attached to a stalk; the grasses nodded; and the white butterfly came blowing this way and that just above her face.

Four feet in the air over her head the apples hung. Suddenly there was a shrill clamour as if they were gongs of cracked brass beaten violently, irregularly and brutally. It was only the schoolchildren saying the multiplication table in unison, stopped by the teacher, scolded and beginning to say the multiplication table over again. But this clamour passed four feet above Miranda's head, went through the apple boughs and, striking against the cowman's little boy, who was picking blackberries in the hedge when he should have been at school, made him tear his thumb on the thorns.

Next there was a solitary cry – sad, human, brutal. Old Parsley was, indeed, blind drunk.

Then the very topmost leaves of the apple tree, flat like little fish against the blue, thirty feet above the earth, chimed with a pensive and lugubrious note. It was the organ in the church playing one of *Hymns Ancient and Modern*. The sound floated out and was cut into atoms by a flock of field-fares flying at an enormous speed – somewhere or other. Miranda lay asleep thirty feet beneath.

Then above the apple tree and the pear tree two hundred feet above Miranda lying asleep in the orchard bells thudded, intermittent, sullen, didactic, for six poor women of the parish were being churched and the Rector was returning thanks to heaven.

And above that with a sharp squeak the golden feather of the church tower turned from south to east. The wind changed. Above everything else it droned, above the woods, the meadows, the hills, miles above Miranda lying in the orchard asleep. It swept on, eyeless, brainless, meeting nothing that could stand against it, until, wheeling the other way, it turned south again. Miles below, in a space as big as the eye of a needle, Miranda stood upright and cried aloud: 'Oh, I shall be late for tea!'

MIRANDA SLEPT in the orchard – or perhaps she was not asleep, for her lips moved very slightly as if they were saying, '*Ce pays est vraiment un des coins du monde... oui le rire des filles... eclate... eclate... eclate,*' and then she smiled and let her body sink all its weight on to the enormous earth which rises, she thought, to carry me on its back as if I were a leaf, or a queen (here the children said the multiplication table), or, Miranda went on, I might be lying on the top of a cliff with the gulls screaming above me. The higher they fly, she continued, as the teacher scolded the children and rapped Jimmy over the knuckles till they bled, the deeper they look into the sea – into the sea, she repeated, and her fingers relaxed and her lips closed gently as if she were floating on the sea, and then, when the shout of the drunken man sounded overhead, she drew breath with an extraordinary ecstasy, for she thought that she heard life itself crying out from a rough tongue in a scarlet mouth, from the wind, from the bells, from the curved green leaves of the cabbages.

Naturally she was being married when the organ played the tune from *Hymns Ancient and Modern*, and, when the bells rang after the six poor women had been churched, the sullen intermittent thud made her think that the very earth shook with the hoofs of the horse that was galloping towards her ('Ah, I have only to wait!' she sighed), and it seemed to her that everything had already begun moving, crying, riding, flying round her, across her, towards her in a pattern.

Mary is chopping the wood, she thought; Pearman is herding the cows; the carts are coming up from the meadows; the rider — and she traced out the lines that the men, the carts, the birds and the rider made over the countryside until they all seemed driven out, round and across by the beat of her own heart.

Miles up in the air the wind changed; the golden feather of the church tower squeaked; and Miranda jumped up and cried: 'Oh, I shall be late for tea!'

MIRANDA SLEPT in the orchard — or was she asleep or was she not asleep? Her purple dress stretched between the two apple trees. There were twenty-four apple trees in the orchard, some slanting slightly, others growing straight with a rush up the trunk which spread wide into branches and formed into round red or yellow drops. Each apple tree had sufficient space. The sky exactly fitted the leaves. When the breeze blew, the line of the boughs against the wall slanted slightly and then returned. A wagtail flew diagonally from one corner to another. Cautiously hopping, a thrush advanced towards a fallen apple; from the other wall a sparrow fluttered just above the grass. The uprush of the trees was tied down by these movements; the whole was compacted by the orchard walls. For

IN THE ORCHARD

miles beneath the earth was clamped together; rippled on the surface with wavering air; and across the corner of the orchard the blue-green was slit by a purple streak. The wind changing, one bunch of apples was tossed so high that it blotted out two cows in the meadow ('Oh, I shall be late for tea!' cried Miranda), and the apples hung straight across the wall again.

THREE PICTURES

The First Picture

IT IS IMPOSSIBLE that one should not see pictures; because if my father was a blacksmith and yours was a peer of the realm, we must needs be pictures to each other. We cannot possibly break out of the frame of the picture by speaking natural words. You see me leaning against the door of the smithy with a horseshoe in my hand and you think as you go by: 'How picturesque!' I, seeing you sitting so much at your ease in the car, almost as if you were going to bow to the populace, think, 'What a picture of old luxurious aristocratical England!' We are both quite wrong in our judgements, no doubt, but that is inevitable.

So now at the turn of the road I saw one of these pictures. It might have been called 'The Sailor's Homecoming' or some such title. A fine young sailor carrying a bundle; a girl with her hand on his arm; neighbours gathering round; a cottage garden ablaze with flowers; as one passed one read at the bottom of that picture that the sailor was back from China, and there was a fine spread waiting for him in the parlour; and he had a present for his young wife in his bundle; and she was soon going to bear him their first child. Everything was right and good and as it should be, one felt about that picture.

There was something wholesome and satisfactory in the sight of such happiness; life seemed sweeter and more enviable than before.

So thinking I passed them, filling in the picture as fully, as completely as I could, noticing the colour of her dress, of his eyes, seeing the sandy cat slinking round the cottage door.

For some time the picture floated in my eyes, making most things appear much brighter, warmer and simpler than usual; and making some things appear foolish; and some things wrong and some things right, and more full of meaning than before. At odd moments during that day and the next the picture returned to one's mind, and one thought with envy, but with kindness, of the happy sailor and his wife; one wondered what they were doing, what they were saying now. The imagination supplied other pictures springing from that first one, a picture of the sailor cutting firewood, drawing water; and they talked about China; and the girl set his present on the chimney piece where everyone who came could see it; and she sewed at her baby clothes, and all the doors and windows were open into the garden so that the birds were flittering and the bees humming, and Rogers – that was his name – could not say how much to his liking all this was after the China seas. As he smoked his pipe, with his foot in the garden.

The Second Picture

IN THE MIDDLE of the night a loud cry rang through the village. Then there was a sound of something scuffling; and then dead silence. All that could be seen out of the window was the branch of lilac tree hanging motionless and ponderous across the road. It was a hot, still night. There was no moon. The cry made everything seem ominous. Who had cried? Why had she cried? It was a woman's voice, made by some extremity of feeling almost sexless, almost expressionless. It was as if human nature had cried out against some iniquity, some inexpressible horror. There was dead silence. The stars shone perfectly steadily. The fields lay still. The trees were motionless. Yet all seemed guilty, convicted, ominous. One felt that something ought to be done. Some

THREE PICTURES

light ought to appear tossing, moving agitatedly. Someone ought to come running down the road. There should be lights in the cottage windows. And then perhaps another cry, but less sexless, less wordless, comforted, appeased. But no light came. No feet were heard. There was no second cry. The first had been swallowed up, and there was dead silence.

One lay in the dark, listening intently. It had been merely a voice. There was nothing to connect it with. No picture of any sort came to interpret it, to make it intelligible to the mind. But as the dark arose at last all one saw was an obscure human form, almost without shape, raising a gigantic arm in vain against some overwhelming iniquity.

The Third Picture

THE FINE WEATHER remained unbroken. Had it not been for that single cry in the night one would have felt that the earth had put into harbour; that life had ceased to drive before the wind; that it had reached some quiet cove and there lay anchored, hardly moving, on the quiet waters. But the sound persisted. Wherever one went, it might be for a long walk up into the hills, something seemed to turn uneasily beneath the surface, making the peace, the stability all round one seem a little unreal. There were the sheep clustered on the side of the hill; the valley broke in long tapering waves like the fall of smooth waters. One came on solitary farmhouses. The puppy rolled in the yard. The butterflies gambolled over the gorse. All was as quiet, as safe could be. Yet, one kept thinking, a cry had rent it; all this beauty had been an accomplice that night; had consented; to remain calm, to be still beautiful; at any moment it might be sundered again. This goodness, this safety were only on the surface.

And then to cheer oneself out of this apprehensive mood one turned to the picture of the sailor's homecoming. One saw it all over again producing various little details – the blue colour of her dress, the shadow that fell from the yellow flowering tree – that one had not used before. So they had stood at the cottage door, he with his bundle on his back, she just lightly touching his sleeve with her hand. And a sandy cat had slunk round the door. Thus gradually going over the picture in every detail, one persuaded oneself by degrees that it was far more likely that this calm and content and goodwill lay beneath the surface than anything treacherous, sinister. The sheep grazing, the waves of the valley, the farmhouse, the puppy, the dancing butterflies were in fact like that all through. And so one turned back home, with one's mind fixed on the sailor and his wife, making up picture after picture of them so that one picture after another of happiness and satisfaction might be laid over that unrest, that hideous cry, until it was crushed and silenced by their pressure out of existence.

Here at last was the village, and the churchyard through which one must pass; and the usual thought came, as one entered it, of the peacefulness of the place, with its shady yews, its rubbed tombstones, its nameless graves. Death is cheerful here, one felt. Indeed, look at that picture! A man was digging a grave, and children were picnicking at the side of it while he worked. As the shovels of yellow earth were thrown up, the children were sprawling about eating bread and jam and drinking milk out of large mugs. The gravedigger's wife, a fat, fair woman, had propped herself against a tombstone and spread her apron on the grass by the open grave to serve as a tea table. Some lumps of clay had fallen among the tea things. Who was going to be buried, I asked. Had old Mr Dodson died at last? 'Oh no! It's for young Rogers, the sailor,' the woman answered, staring at me. 'He died two nights ago, of some foreign fever. Didn't you hear his wife?' She rushed into the road and cried out, 'Here, Tommy, you're all covered with earth!'

What a picture it made!

EVENING OVER SUSSEX

REFLECTIONS IN A MOTOR CAR

EVENING IS KIND to Sussex, for Sussex is no longer young, and she is grateful for the veil of evening as an elderly woman is glad when a shade is drawn over a lamp, and only the outline of her face remains. The outline of Sussex is still very fine. The cliffs stand out to sea, one behind another. All Eastbourne, all Bexhill, all St Leonards, their parades and their lodging houses, their bead shops and their sweet shops and their placards and their invalids and charabancs,* are all obliterated. What remains is what there was when William came over from France ten centuries ago: a line of cliffs running out to sea. Also the fields are redeemed. The freckle of red villas on the coast is washed over by a thin lucid lake of brown air, in which they and their redness are drowned. It was still too early for lamps; and too early for stars.

But, I thought, there is always some sediment of irritation when the moment is as beautiful as it is now. The psychologists must explain; one looks up, one is overcome by beauty extravagantly greater than one could expect – there are now pink clouds over Battle; the fields are mottled, marbled – one's perceptions blow out rapidly like air balls expanded by some rush of air, and then, when all seems blown to its fullest and tautest, with beauty and beauty and beauty, a pin pricks; it collapses. But what is the pin? So far as I could tell, the pin had something to do with one's own impotency. I cannot hold this – I cannot express this – I am overcome by it – I am mastered. Somewhere in that region one's discontent lay; and it was allied with the idea that one's nature demands mastery over all that it receives; and mastery here meant the power to convey what one saw now over Sussex so that another person could share it. And further, there was another prick of the pin: one was wasting one's chance; for beauty spread at one's right hand, at one's left; at one's back, too; it was escaping all the time; one could only offer a thimble to a torrent that could fill baths, lakes.

But relinquish, I said (it is well known how in circumstances like these the self splits up and one self is eager and dissatisfied and the other stern and philosophical), relinquish these impossible aspirations; be content with the view in front of us, and believe me when I tell you that it is best to sit and soak; to be passive; to accept; and do not bother because nature has given you six little pocket knives with which to cut up the body of a whale.

While these two selves then held a colloquy about the wise course to adopt in the presence of beauty, I (a third party now declared itself) said to myself, how happy they were to enjoy so simple an occupation. There they sat as the car sped along, noticing everything: a hay stack; a rust-red roof; a pond; an old man coming home with his sack on his back; there they sat, matching every colour in the sky and earth from their colour box, rigging up little models of Sussex barns and farmhouses in the red light that would serve in the January gloom. But I, being somewhat different, sat aloof and melancholy. While they are thus busied, I said to myself: Gone, gone; over, over; past and done with, past and done with. I feel life left behind even as the road is left behind. We have been over that stretch, and are already forgotten. There, windows were lit by our lamps for a second; the light is out now. Others come behind us.

Then suddenly a fourth self (a self which lies in ambush, apparently dormant, and jumps upon one unawares. Its remarks are often entirely disconnected with what has been happening, but must be attended to because of their very abruptness) said: 'Look at that.' It was a light; brilliant, freakish; inexplicable. For a second I was unable to name it. 'A star'; and for that second it held its odd flicker of unexpectedness and danced and beamed. 'I take your meaning,' I said. 'You, erratic and impulsive self that you are, feel that the light over the downs there emerging, dangles from the future. Let us try to understand this. Let us reason it out. I feel suddenly attached not to the past but to the future. I think of Sussex in five hundred years to come. I think much grossness will have evaporated. Things will have been scorched up, eliminated. There will be magic gates. Draughts fan-blown by electric power will cleanse houses. Lights intense and firmly directed will go over the earth, doing the work. Look at the moving light in that hill; it is the headlight of a car. By day and by night Sussex in five centuries will be full of charming thoughts, quick, effective beams.'

EVENING OVER SUSSEX

The sun was now low beneath the horizon. Darkness spread rapidly. None of my selves could see anything beyond the tapering light of our headlamps on the hedge. I summoned them together. 'Now,' I said, 'comes the season of making up our accounts. Now we have got to collect ourselves; we have got to be one self. Nothing is to be seen any more, except one wedge of road and bank which our lights repeat incessantly. We are perfectly provided for. We are warmly wrapped in a rug; we are protected from wind and rain. We are alone. Now is the time of reckoning. Now I, who preside over the company, am going to arrange in order the trophies which we have all brought in. Let me see; there was a great deal of beauty brought in today: farmhouses; cliffs standing out to sea; marbled fields; mottled fields; red feathered skies; all that. Also there was disappearance and the death of the individual. The vanishing road and the window lit for a second and then dark. And then there was the sudden dancing light, that was hung in the future. What we have made then today,' I said, 'is this: that beauty; death of the individual; and the future. Look, I will make a little figure for your satisfaction; here he comes. Does this little figure advancing through beauty, through death, to the economical, powerful and efficient future when houses will be cleansed by a puff of hot wind satisfy you? Look at him; there on my knee.' We sat and looked at the figure we had made that day. Great sheer slabs of rock, tree tufted, surrounded him. He was for a second very, very solemn. Indeed it seemed as if the reality of things were displayed there on the rug. A violent thrill ran through us; as if a charge of electricity had entered in to us. We cried out together: 'Yes, yes,' as if affirming something, in a moment of recognition.

And then the body who had been silent up to now began its song, almost at first as low as the rush of the wheels: 'Eggs and bacon; toast and tea; fire and a bath; fire and a bath; jugged hare,' it went on, 'and redcurrant jelly; a glass of wine with coffee to follow, with coffee to follow – and then to bed and then to bed.'

'Off with you,' I said to my assembled selves. 'Your work is done. I dismiss you. Goodnight.'

And the rest of the journey was performed in the delicious society of my own body.

NOTES

Although 'In the Orchard' was written in 1923, it was not published until April 1923, when it appeared in *The Criterion*. Likewise, while 'Three Pictures' was composed in June 1929, it was not committed to print until 1942, when it appeared, along with 'Evening Over Sussex: Reflections in a Motor Car', in *The Death of the Moth and Other Essays*. In some instances, spelling, punctuation and grammar have been silently corrected to make the text more appealing to the modern reader.

9 *Ce pays est vraiment… le mieux*: Woolf is quoting here from the 1897 French novel *Ramuntcho* by Pierre Loti (1850–1923). (In English: 'Truly, this country is one of the corners of the world where girls burst into laughter most readily…')

29 *charabancs*: A type of early coach, used for pleasure trips.

A Biographical Note on

Virginia Woolf

Adeline Virginia Stephen was born into the affluent Stephen family in Kensington on the 25th of January 1882. Woolf was the seventh of eight children in a blended family; her mother, Julia Prinsep Jackson, a Pre-Raphaelite model and philanthropist, and her father, Leslie Stephen, an author, literary critic and the first Editor of the Dictionary of National Biography, had had four children in previous marriages. Of her siblings, Virginia is the best known today, although her sister Vanessa Bell, the Modernist painter, who provided the illustrations to many of Virginia's works, is still highly thought of, and her half-brother Gerald Duckworth (from Julia's first marriage) founded the successful Gerald Duckworth and Company publishing house.

Most of the Stephen family's life was spent at their elegant town house, 22 Hyde Park Gate, as well as at the country estate, Talland House, in Cornwall, where the family visited Godrevy Lighthouse, which would eventually become the inspiration for *To the Lighthouse*. Of her childhood, Woolf wrote that she was 'born into a large connection, born not of rich parents, but of well-to-do parents, born into a very communicative, literate, letter-writing, visiting, articulate, late-nineteenth-century world', and it was in this setting that the children were given a taste of distinguished company.

Leslie Stephen's importance in the literary world and his connection to William Makepeace Thackeray (his first marriage was to the author's daughter, Harriet), as well as Julia Stephen's popularity and philanthropy, meant that the London home was frequently filled with literary royalty, including Henry James, George Meredith, Thomas Hardy and Alfred, Lord Tennyson. No doubt it was being surrounded by writers of such prowess, as well as an unfettered access to her father's impressive library, that set Woolf on the path to becoming a writer. While her parents didn't approve of education for women, they did approve of her writing, and she later described being encouraged to write 'ever since I was a little creature, scribbling a story in the manner of Hawthorne on the green plush sofa in the drawing room at St Ives while the grown-ups dined…'

Woolf spoke fondly of her early childhood – particularly of the time spent at Talland House – but was forced to grow up suddenly when, in 1895, her mother fell ill with influenza, and died in May from the complications it brought with it. The loss of her mother affected the thirteen-year-old Virginia greatly, and she suffered a mental breakdown, which marked the beginning of her suffering with mental illness.

Stella, Woolf's half-sister, returned home to take on the role of mother to Virginia and Vanessa. Two years later, however, she died, too, and Woolf was left reeling. She later wrote of this time that the family had suffered 'the lash of a random unheeding flail that pointlessly and brutally killed the two people who should, normally and naturally, have made those years not, perhaps, happy, but normal and natural.' During this period, Woolf later said, she had also been subjected to sexual molestation by her half-brother

George, from as early an age as six; it is clear that the events unsurprisingly left the young Virginia scarred.

A mere five years later, Leslie Stephen fell ill, and died soon after, in 1904, administering another blow to the young Virginia and precipitating another mental breakdown. Little about the family was recorded during this period, so not much is known about Woolf's breakdown, except that it took her about three months to recover, and it is thought that she attempted to commit suicide.

At about this time, Woolf's literary career began to take root – while she wasn't permitted to join her brothers, Thoby and Adrian, at Oxbridge universities, they introduced their sisters to their circle of friends, which included Lytton Strachey and Leonard Woolf. In the mean time, able to pursue a formal education at last, Virginia enrolled at the Ladies' Department of King's College, London, where she studied Ancient Greek, Latin and German. Her tutors, Janet Case and Clara Pater, introduced her to the women's rights movement. She also met several leading education reformists, such as the Principal of the Ladies' Department, Lilian Faithfull.

NOTES

After their parents' death, Vanessa and Virginia decided to sell up and move to somewhere new. Uncertain of their financial future, they moved to 46 Gordon Square in Bloomsbury, which was a relatively cheap and bohemian area at that time. Here, they began to entertain Thoby's university friends, including writers and literary critics such as Lytton Strachey, Clive Bell and Desmond MacCarthy. The group grew in size and expanded into what became known as the Bloomsbury Set, which also included John Maynard Keynes, E.M. Forster, Roger Fry and Leonard Woolf.

Only a year later, in 1906, Thoby died; the following year, Vanessa married Clive Bell and moved out, leaving the last two siblings, Virginia and Adrian, to look for a new home. That April, they moved to 29 Fitzroy Square – not far from Gordon Square. This period was marked with difficulty, however; when travelling with Vanessa and her husband, Virginia found herself very interested in Clive Bell, and a rivalry between the sisters sprang up. Eventually, when the lease on the Fitzroy Square house ran out, she and Adrian moved to 38 Brunswick Square with John Maynard Keynes and Duncan Grant, incurring the disapproval of the Duckworth side of the family.

41

From July 1911, Virginia began to spend more time with Leonard Woolf, who had moved into the top floor of the Brunswick Square house. Despite her initial objections to marriage, they were wed in 1912, and moved to a new house together. During this period, Virginia continued to work on her first novel, *The Voyage Out*, while struggling with mental illness again, culminating in another suicide attempt in 1913. Leonard sought advice from medical professionals, and eventually decided that it would be best for Virginia to convalesce, so they moved to Richmond, then in the Surrey countryside, in 1914.

Over the next year, Virginia took a turn for the worse; she was still working on *The Voyage Out*, and, though having secured a promise of publication, her dread of its negative reception added to her mental unrest.

In the mean time, of course, the First World War was looming in the background, and the following year, 1916, saw the introduction of conscription. Leonard was spared on medical grounds, as he described in a letter: 'I am in great trouble about conscription. I shall, of course, apply for exemption on grounds of health – (shaking hands) and domestic hardship.' Thus the Woolfs were spared a first-hand experience of the war; none the less, it cast a shadow over much of Virginia's later work, playing an important role in the background of many of her novels.

From a young age, Virginia had enjoyed book-binding, and she and Leonard dreamt of setting up a press of their own. In 1917 the dream became a reality: they bought a hand press, which they put on the dining-room table and began to teach themselves to make books, and founded Hogarth Press, named after their new house in Richmond. They were able to publish *Two Stories*, which contained 'The Mark on the Wall' by Virginia and 'Three Jews' by Leonard, a mere three months later. Other works soon followed, including short stories by Virginia, such as *Kew Gardens*, with woodblock illustrations by Vanessa Bell. The press soon gained traction, and they started to publish works by Clive Bell, Roger Fry, John Maynard Keynes, T.S. Eliot, Edith Sitwell, Maxim Gorky and many more. This was a crucial step for Virginia – the means of production, of course, being tantamount to control over every aspect of her works.

In 1916 Vanessa Bell took on the Charleston Farmhouse near the Sussex coast as a summer house; it soon became the scene for a revival of the Bloomsbury Set, its members having been scattered after the war. Three years later the Woolfs followed suit, buying the Round House in Lewes, which they promptly re-sold in favour of the Monk's House in nearby Rodmell, which came with an acre of land and a view across the River Ouse towards the South Downs.

The next few years saw a great literary output from Virginia, starting with a short-story collection, *Monday or Tuesday* (1921), a novel, *Night and Day* (1922) and the novel *Jacob's Room* (1922).

It was later that year that Virginia met 'the lovely gifted aristocratic [Vita] Sackville-West', a successful writer, poet and gardener. Virginia was immediately drawn to Vita, and the two entered a relationship which would last for many years, eventually evolving into a deep friendship. Vita was good for Virginia, helping her to improve her sense of self-worth, and to see reading and writing as positive, rather than detrimental to her health, as doctors had previously suggested.

In 1924, the Woolfs moved back to Bloomsbury, taking on 52 Tavistock Square, from which they continued to run the Hogarth Press, and in which Virginia had a writing room – a room of her own. This period was also rich in literary output, and saw the publication of *Mrs Dalloway* (1925), *To the Lighthouse* (1927) and *Orlando* (1928).

It was at this point that Woolf's political ideas became more prominent: in October 1928 she gave two talks on 'women and fiction' at Newnham and Girton colleges, which led to the publication of *A Room of One's Own* the following year, and, soon after, 'Professions for Women' (1931).

Woolf now began work on her most stylistically innovative novel, *The Waves*. This was due in no small part to Vita Sackville-West publishing her books through the Hogarth Press, helping to make the press profitable and allowing Virginia to be more experimental in her writing.

In 1937, the international situation worsened again, which affected Virginia greatly – both due to her deep-set horror of war and also the death of her nephew, Vanessa's son Julian, who was killed in the Spanish Civil War. Virginia began to work on a treatise against war, *Three Guineas*, an indictment of Fascism and a portrayal of violence as a patriarchal tool.

As old friends – such as Roger Fry – died, and war loomed, her final years were darkened by tragedy. Her writing suffered as a result, as she began to doubt her abilities, but she still managed to write *Between the Acts*. In 1939 the Woolfs moved again within London, to 37 Mecklenburgh Square, but the house was destroyed during the Blitz in September 1940, so they moved permanently to Monk House in Sussex.

The couple were under immense strain – Virginia was isolated from her friends and filled with grief, and Britain feared immanent invasion by Hitler, which was all the more concerning as Leonard was Jewish. Her mental state grew worse, and on the 28th of March 1941 she filled her pockets with rocks and walked into the River Ouse, leaving a moving note to Leonard, which is now almost as well known as her books:

> Dearest, I feel certain that I am going mad again. I feel we can't go through another of those terrible times. And I shan't recover this time. I begin to hear voices, and I can't concentrate. So I am doing what seems the best thing to do. You have given me the greatest possible happiness. You have been in every way all that anyone could be. I don't think two people could have been happier till

this terrible disease came. I can't fight it any longer. I know that I am spoiling your life, that without me you could work. And you will I know. You see I can't even write this properly. I can't read. What I want to say is I owe all the happiness of my life to you. You have been entirely patient with me and incredibly good. I want to say that – everybody knows it. If anybody could have saved me it would have been you. Everything has gone from me but the certainty of your goodness. I can't go on spoiling your life any longer. I don't think two people could have been happier than we have been. V.

ALSO AVAILABLE BY VIRGINIA WOOLF

THE VIRGINIA WOOLF COLLECTION
beautiful editions of the major works with gold-foiled covers

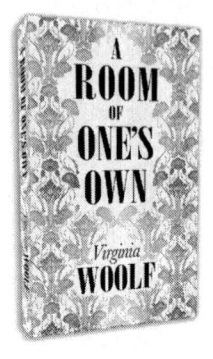

ISBN: 9781913724009
Paperback • £7.99 • 160pp

ISBN: 9781913724726
Paperback • £7.99 • 208pp

ISBN: 9781913724092
Paperback • £7.99 • 224pp

IN THE SAME FORMAT

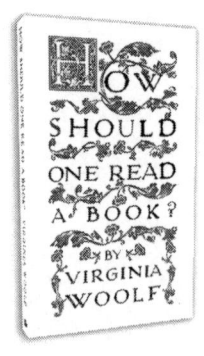

ISBN: 9781913724474
48pp • Paperback • £3

ISBN: 9781804470312
48pp • Paperback • £3

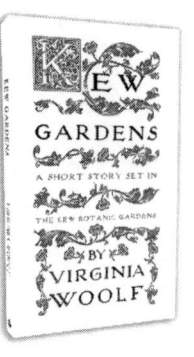

ISBN: 9781913724122
48pp • Paperback • £3

WWW.RENARDPRESS.COM